Lots of
love and.
best wishes
Marie Archi

Laurie Archi

SUKI & Mirabella

Carmela & Steven D'Amico

DIAL BOOKS FOR YOUNG READERS

An imprint of Penguin Group (USA) Inc.

For the one-and-only, brilliant Olivia

DIAL BOOKS FOR YOUNG READERS
A division of Penguin Young Readers Group
Published by the Penguin Group
Penguin Group (USA) Inc., 375 Hudson Street, New York, New York 10014, U.S.A.
Penguin Group (Canada), 90 Eglinton Avenue East, Suite 700, Toronto, Ontario, Canada M4P 2Y3 (a division of
Pearson Penguin Canada Inc.) • Penguin Books Ltd, 80 Strand, London WC2R 0RL, England • Penguin Ireland,
25 St Stephen's Green, Dublin 2, Ireland (a division of Penguin Books Ltd) • Penguin Group (Australia), 250
Camberwell Road, Camberwell, Victoria 3124, Australia (a division of Pearson Australia Group Pty Ltd) •
Penguin Books India Pvt Ltd, 11 Community Centre, Panchsheel Park, New Delhi - 110 017, India • Penguin
Group (NZ), 67 Apollo Drive, Rosedale, Auckland 0632, New Zealand (a division of Pearson New Zealand Ltd)
• Penguin Books (South Africa) (Pty) Ltd, 24 Sturdee Avenue, Rosebank, Johannesburg 2196, South Africa •
Penguin Books Ltd, Registered Offices : 80 Strand, London WC2R 0RL, England

Text set in Pabst Oldstyle
Manufactured in China on acid-free paper

10 9 8 7 6 5 4 3 2 1

Library of Congress Cataloging-in-Publication Data
D'Amico, Carmela.
 Suki and Mirabella / Carmela & Steven D'Amico. -- 1st ed.
    p. cm.
 Summary : Suki, a bunny who likes being the center of attention, loses
her followers when cousin Mirabella arrives.
 ISBN 978-0-8037-3740-2 (hardcover)
 [1. Rabbits--Fiction. 2. Cousins--Fiction. 3. Behavior--Fiction.] I.
D'Amico, Steven. II. Title.
 PZ7.D1837Sr 2013
 [E]--dc23   2012017681

The pictures for *Suki & Mirabella* were created with charcoal pencils on Rives BFK paper,
scanned into a 27`` iMac and colored using custom digital charcoal tools in Corel Painter 12.

In the burrows where Suki lived nothing much ever changed. There were always lots of dandelions to eat. She always got plenty of attention from Momma. And she always taught her brothers and sisters the fun games she made up.

One morning, they were playing Suki, Queen of the Maple Tree Grove. Again.

Suki didn't think Mickey was doing a very good
job getting the court to bow when she hopped onto her
throne. "I'm tired of this game," he said.
"Then let's play bumblebees!" Suki shouted.
"Why, so you can be queen again?"

Suddenly, there was noise and excitement coming
from the burrows.

"Hey, where's everyone going," Suki called as her
brothers and sisters scurried off.

Out of curiosity Suki followed them.

"This is your cousin Mirabella," Momma said.
"She's visiting us for the summer."
Suki bounded through the huddle and shouted,
"Hi! I'm Suki! We were just in the middle of a game.
Wanna play? We can play bumblebees!"

"No thanks," said Mirabella. "I don't like getting dirty."

"It's fun," Suki said.

"Maybe it's fun for you. But my coat is very shiny. And I like to keep it that way."

"Boring," Suki said, and she started to hop away, expecting her brothers and sisters to follow. But they circled Mirabella, excitedly asking her questions.

"Come on everyone!" she shouted. "Let's go back to our game!"

"But nobody wants to play bumblebees, remember?" Mickey said.

"What do you want to play?"
Mirabella asked Mickey.

His eyes lit up. "Well, there's
a hollow around the bend that's
perfect for hide-and-seek. It's not
muddy so your coat will stay clean."
"I love hide-and-seek!" she said.

And suddenly everyone was
hopping after Mickey and Mirabella.
Except for Suki.

"Why aren't you playing with the others?" Momma asked.

"Hide-and-seek is boring."

"Only boring bunnies get bored. And if there's one thing I know about you, Suki, you can make anything fun. Besides, I need you to go and tell everyone lunch will be ready soon."

Suki wasn't feeling very fun, but she knew Momma was usually right.

On her way to the hollow, she spotted one of her favorite old toys. Of all her brothers and sisters, Suki could roll the longest and fastest.

She bet Mirabella with her shiny coat and fancy name couldn't do that.

"Look out!" Suki shouted.

"Shhh! Be quiet. I'm hiding,"
Mickey said. "Mirabella's *it*."

"Oh! We have one of those on the farm!"
Mirabella said.

"I bet I can go faster than you," Suki
challenged.

Mirabella laughed. "I don't use it to
go anywhere, silly!"

"Well, I don't like to do stuff if I have to stay in one spot," Suki said. "That's boring. I like to run as fast as the wind and hop as high as the sky! Like this!"

"I can hop higher than any other animal on the farm," said Mirabella. "Even the cat!"

"Well, I bet
you can't do . . .

. . . this,"
Suki said.

"But I can do this," said Mirabella.

"Voilà!" she
said with a bow.

Nobody moved or spoke until Mickey
declared, "Let's have a contest!"

"Whoever finds the crown first," Mickey said, "wins."

"But that's my crown!" Suki shouted.
"I didn't see your name on it," Mirabella said.
"Aren't you afraid of getting dirty?" Suki
teased as she dashed toward the bushes.

"Got it!"
they shouted at once.

"A tie!" Mirabella exclaimed.

"Now look what you've done!" Suki
shouted. "I'm telling Momma!"

"Go ahead!"

But when Suki tried to move,
she realized she was stuck.
"Wait for me!" she called.

Pushing through the thicket, Mirabella said,
"I know what you need to do. Just pull your left leg
up, then wiggle your left arm free, then . . . then . . .
oh, no! Now I'm stuck, too!"

Suki giggled.

"It's not funny," Mirabella said.

"It's kind of funny," said Suki.

"Is not."

"Is too."

"Is not," said Mirabella, but she started giggling, too.

"I know what we need to do," Suki said, and reached for Mirabella.

"I'm sorry your coat got dirty," Suki said.

"I'm sorry your crown broke," Mirabella said.

"It's not a crown," Suki said. . . .

"Look! It's two tiaras!"

"Who won?" Mickey asked.

"We both did!"
Suki and Mirabella said together.

Darcey Sills

"I'm Owen," Dwight's uncle says, as he walks along the beach with us, carrying his red metal toolbox.

"Hey O," Dwight says. "This gal's in trouble. She's got a plastic bag stuck over her neck and it looks like she's got some in her mouth, too."

Owen puts the toolbox down and kneels in the soft sand by the turtle's head. The turtle is too tangled to pull her head inside her shell and she's too tired to move. Her mouth slowly opens and closes but she's as still as a rock.

◀ Loretta Rogers

23

I run my hand along the bumpy ridges of the turtle's shell. "What kind is it?" I ask.

"She's a Hawksbill Turtle," Dwight says. "Her shell is called a carapace and it's hard with this unique pattern of colorful overlapping scales. Hawksbills aren't the biggest turtles in the ocean, but they can weigh up to 150 pounds. They get their name from their long heads that taper to a point, like a bird's bill. See?"

Snip. Owen uses scissors to make the first cut on the plastic bag. Snip. The second cut frees the bag from around its head. Then Dwight carefully opens the turtle's mouth and pulls out the rest of the plastic.

Loretta Rogers

◄ Susan Gosevitz

25

"It's a good thing that bag didn't choke her," Dwight says. "I bet the poor thing thought it was a sponge, her favorite food, and tried to eat it. These turtles are endangered, which means there aren't many of them left and they could become extinct if we don't protect them."

"How did a plastic bag get all the way out here?" Chloe asks.

"When people throw their trash away, a lot of it ends up in the sea. It's killing our oceans and its creatures," Dwight says.

Owen goes to the lighthouse to call for help. When he returns he says, "The Marine Animal Rescue Centre will be here in an hour."

Teagan — that's what I've named the turtle — makes a tiny wiggle with her back right fin but other than that she's still.

Susan Gosevitz

◀ Loretta Rogers

As Teagan rests, I lay my head on Mom's shoulder and gaze out to the ocean. My eyelids are heavy but I don't want to sleep. Suddenly I hear a giant splash.

"What was that?" I ask. Everyone turns to look as two light gray dolphins emerge from the water. "Those, my friends, are Bottlenose Dolphins," Dwight says, smiling.

Just then a Brown Pelican dives toward the water, scooping a fish into its beak before flying off. This amazing ocean is filled with life.

The sun is setting when the rescue crew arrives and hoists Teagan into their boat. "Your quick thinking helped save this turtle," one of them says as he pats me on the head.

◀ Loretta Rogers

Robert Bateman

Loretta Rogers

We've been home from Nassau for a month when Dad calls us into the kitchen. He's sitting in front of his laptop at the table. Dwight's big smile fills the screen.

"Here she is," he says. "We're about to release Teagan back into the ocean. It took a while, but she's completely healed and ready to go home."

Now it's Teagan that fills the screen. A small scar runs around her neck, but other than that she looks healthy. We watch quietly as she slowly waddles into the water.

I hold Chloe's hand as Teagan gets smaller and smaller. She seems to wave a flipper at us as if to say goodbye before she disappears beneath the waves and heads back to the coral reef.

Darcey Sills ▶

Did You Know?

Things made of **plastic**, such as shopping bags and bottles, make up more than 60 percent of ocean pollution. Many of these items, especially plastic bags, can block the breathing passages and stomachs of ocean animals like seals, dolphins, whales and turtles. The plastic rings found around six-packs of pop cans can also be deadly, choking the creatures unlucky enough to get their heads stuck through the holes.

The **Hawksbill Turtle** got its name from its narrow head and hawk-like beak. It feeds mainly on sponges that live on coral reefs. It is a critically endangered species, largely due to people taking its colorful shell to sell in markets.

A group of **jellyfish** is called a smack. Jellyfish consist of 95 percent water, they don't have a head, heart, brain or skeleton and they've existed for millions of years – long before the dinosaurs.

Algae is the favorite food of the brightly colored **Parrot Fish**. They use teeth in their throats to help grind and crush coral to remove the algae.

The bits they don't digest get pooped out and turn into soft, white sand.

Oceans make up 71 percent of the earth's surface and contain 97 percent of the world's water. Over three quarters of the oceans' pollution comes from land. Oil, sewage, fertilizers and garbage are some of the major threats to marine wildlife and coral reefs.

Coral reefs around the world support up to two million species, including fish, sponges and crustaceans like crabs and shrimp. Reefs are made up of plants and tiny invertebrate animals called polyps. Today, coral reefs are being threatened by global warming, dynamite fishing, garbage, oil, sewage and mining. You can kill coral just by touching it.

Lobsters are only red once they're cooked. They come in many different colors, including blue. They taste with their legs and are able to regrow their limbs.

The **Yellow-Crowned Night Heron** has bad manners. He swallows his dinner of crabs and crayfish whole

– without chewing! He doesn't sleep much, either, as he likes to be active during the day and night.

Dolphins are mammals, not fish. That means they are warm-blooded, breathe air and give birth to live young. A female dolphin is called a cow, a male is a bull and their babies are called calves.

Brown Surgeonfish are peaceful and friendly – unless you try to eat their algae. Whether the algae's on a piece of coral or on a turtle's shell, these fish get very territorial about their feeding grounds.

Green Sea Turtles love to sunbathe to stay warm. They can often be found soaking up the sun's rays on a sandy beach.

Fantastic at camouflaging themselves, **Lion Fish** have super-fast reflexes. If you manage to get close to one, don't touch it! Their sting is painful and can cause nausea, breathing problems and sometimes paralysis.